BEWARE THE
INQUISITOR!

Written by Lisa Stock

Written and Edited by Lisa Stock
Editor Anant Sagar
Art Editor Radhika Banerjee
Managing Editors Laura Gilbert,
Chitra Subramanyam
Managing Art Editors Maxine Pedliham,
Neha Ahuja
Art Director Lisa Lanzarini
DTP Designer Umesh Singh Rawat
Pre-Production Producer Marc Staples,
Pre-Production Manager Sunil Sharma
Producer David Appleyard
Reading Consultant Maureen Fernandes

Publisher Julie Ferris
Publishing Director Simon Beecroft

For Lucasfilm
Executive Editor Jonathan W. Rinzler
Art Director Troy Alders
Story Group Rayne Roberts, Pablo Hidalgo, Leland Chee

First published in Great Britain in 2015 by
Dorling Kindersley Limited
80 Strand, London, WC2R 0RL

Page design copyright © 2015 Dorling Kindersley Limited
A Penguin Random House Company
10 9 8 7 6 5 4 3 2
002–270977–Jan/15

Copyright © 2014 Lucasfilms Ltd. and ™

A CIP catalogue record for this book
is available from the British Library.
ISBN: 978-0-24118-532-2

Colour reproduction by Alta Image Ltd, UK
Printed and bound in China by South China Printing Company Ltd.

www.starwars.com
www.dk.com

A WORLD OF IDEAS:
SEE ALL THERE IS TO KNOW

Contents

4   Who is the Inquisitor?

6   Inquisitor Fact File

8   Lothal

10 Rebel Trouble

12 Wanted!

14 Imperial Army

16 Stormtrooper Armour

18 Lothal's Imperial Academy

20 Serving the Empire

22 Imperial Navy

24 Secret Agent

26 Jedi Alert

28 Space Chases

30 TIE Advanced

32 Capturing Jedi

34 Ezra's Guide

36 Great Escape

38 Mission Report

40 Inquisitor's Anger

42 Quiz

44 Glossary

45 Index

46 Guide for Parents

Who is the Inquisitor?

This scary alien is the Inquisitor. He is from the planet Utapau. The Inquisitor works for the evil Empire that controls the galaxy. He is on the hunt for Jedi who are in hiding.

THE INQUISITOR

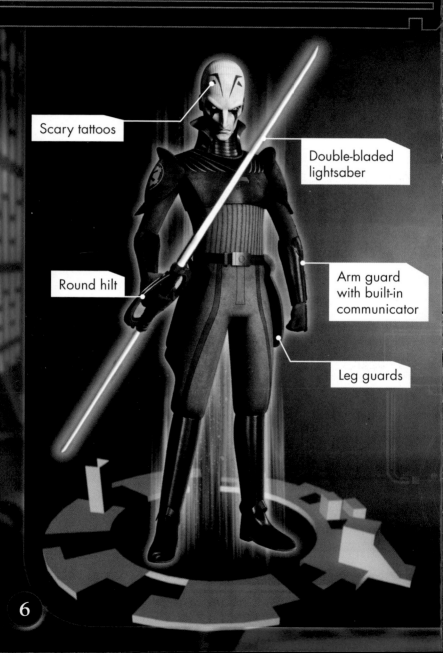

Scary tattoos

Double-bladed lightsaber

Round hilt

Arm guard with built-in communicator

Leg guards

FACT FILE

CODE NAME: INQUISITOR

OCCUPATION: JEDI HUNTER

DISTINCTIVE MARK: RED TATTOOS

WEAPON: LIGHTSABER

STRENGTHS

- POWERFUL IN COMBAT
- FEROCIOUS LIGHTSABER FIGHTER
- INTELLIGENT AND CUNNING
- CREATES DEADLY TRAPS

NO LISTED WEAKNESSES!

Lothal

The planet of Lothal is very important to the Empire because it is rich in minerals. The Empire does not put up with trouble there.
Any rebellion is quickly stamped out.

Rebel Trouble

On Lothal, six rebels have joined together.

They do not like being ruled by the Empire and they are fighting back!

But beware: the Inquisitor is
after the rebels because he knows
that one of them is a Jedi.

Any information on these rebels must be reported to the nearest Imperial Outpost.

ZEB ORRELIOS

WANTED

For injuring Imperial stormtroopers.

EZRA BRIDGER

WANTED

For stealing helmets from the Imperial army and training as a Jedi.

HERA SYNDULLA

WANTED

For beating the Empire's TIE fighters in a space chase.

KANAN JARRUS

WANTED

For being a Jedi and
using a lightsaber.
Approach with caution!

SABINE WREN

WANTED

For blowing up Imperial property
with graffiti bombs.

CHOPPER

WANTED

For aggressive attitude
and leaking oil on
Imperial property.

Imperial Army

The Inquisitor is helped by the Empire's army of stormtroopers. These loyal soldiers are trained to protect the Empire at any cost. They spread fear and terror across the galaxy.

STORMTROOPER ARMOUR

Standard blaster

Helmet

Shoulder guard

Chest plate

Utility belt

Suit controls

Power cell

Knee guard

Tough shoes

A stormtrooper's armour is fitted with many clever gadgets. These gadgets help the stormtroopers survive their dangerous missions.

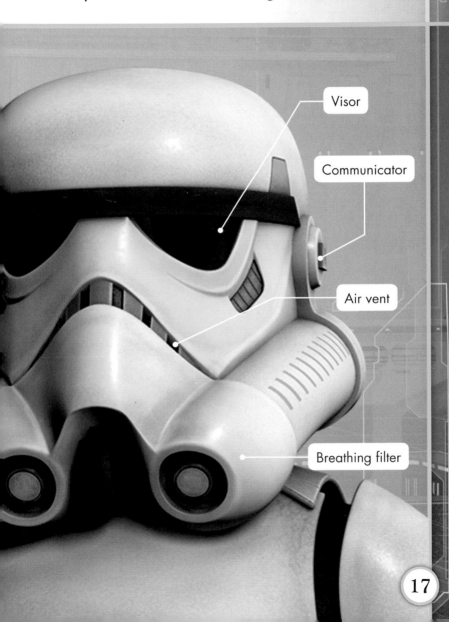

Visor

Communicator

Air vent

Breathing filter

Lothal's Imperial Academy

Taskmaster Grint and Commandant Aresko are in charge of training stormtrooper cadets.

The training takes place at Lothal's Imperial Academy. The two agents are cruel and quite foolish, too!

SERVING THE EMPIRE

Top tips

from the galaxy's toughest officers

Jedi Hunter

⚙ TRAINING TIP

Learn to feel the Force and never trust the Jedi.

Secret Police Agent

✦ TRAINING TIP

When tracking rebels, remember to shoot first and ask questions later.

Cadet Trainer

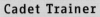 TRAINING TIP

Always be on the lookout for traitors to the Empire.

Stormtrooper

TRAINING TIP

Practise at the shooting range whenever you can.

TIE Pilot

TRAINING TIP

Remember to follow your orders and always stick to the plan!

Lothal Academy Teacher

TRAINING TIP

Failure is not acceptable! The Empire has no time for weakness.

21

Imperial Navy

The Empire has a fleet
of powerful spaceships.
The most powerful ship
is the Star Destroyer.
It can wipe out a whole
city with one blast.
A Star Destroyer looms
over Lothal.

Secret Agent

Agent Kallus is an officer
of the secret police.
His job is to check that
everyone is following
the Empire's rules.
He discovers that there
are Jedi on Lothal.
This is a job for the Inquisitor!

JEDI ALERT

Agent Kallus knows that he cannot fight the rebels alone. He must call the Inquisitor for help.

SECURE CALL CONNECTED TO
THE INQUISITOR

"Excuse the intrusion, Inquisitor. But in the course of my duties, I have encountered a rebel cell. The leader of the cell made good use of a lightsaber."

SECURE CALL FROM
AGENT KALLUS

"Ah, Agent Kallus.
You did well to call.
Now tell me everything
you know about this Jedi."

Space Chases

The Empire's TIE fighter
spaceships are nimble
and very fast.

The Inquisitor flies a
special version named
the TIE Advanced.
This ship is perfect for his
top-secret missions.

TIE ADVANCED

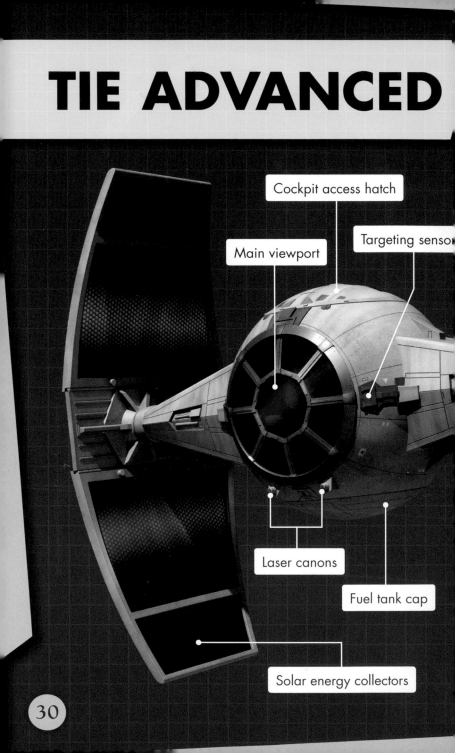

Cockpit access hatch

Targeting sensor

Main viewport

Laser canons

Fuel tank cap

Solar energy collectors

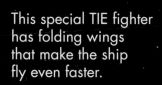

This special TIE fighter
has folding wings
that make the ship
fly even faster.

Length: 9.2 m (30 feet)

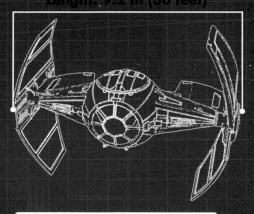

Speed: 1,600 Km/h (960 mph)

Ships destroyed: 42

Missile capacity: 20 shells

Capturing Jedi

The Jedi use a special power
called the Force.
The Inquisitor can also
feel the Force.

This means he knows
when a Jedi is near.
He has many tricks and traps
to catch his victims.
There is no place to hide!

PLANNING AN ESCAPE

Ezra's step-by-step guide

1

If an Imperial officer catches you, don't panic!
Make sure you don't let him see that you are afraid.

2

Find a disguise and hide in the air vents.
Stormtrooper helmets have radios. Be sneaky and listen in.

3

Your friends are sure to come to your rescue. Run to your ship as fast as you can, but watch out for stormtroopers.

4

Need a distraction?
A big explosion is perfect to keep the Empire off your back while you make your exit.

Great Escape

The Inquisitor lures the rebels into a trap!
He thinks it will be easy to defeat them.
But the Jedi rebel named Kanan is very brave.
He fights with the Inquisitor until all the rebels manage to escape.

INQUISITOR'S
MISSION REPORT

MISSION TARGET
Capture rebels on Lothal

MISSION RESULT
FAILURE

Reason for failure:

- Rebels are smarter than expected

- Stormtroopers were beaten

- Traps did not work as planned

- Rebel ship could not be tracked

ANOTHER PLAN IS NEEDED...

Inquisitor's Anger

The rebels were able to
escape this time.
However, they are
not entirely safe.
The Inquisitor is
very angry that he
has failed his mission.
He will not give up
until he has captured
every last Jedi.
Watch out, rebels!

Quiz

1. Which planet is the Inquisitor from?

2. Who is the Inquisitor trying to catch?

3. Which planet is important to the Empire?

4. What are Imperial soldiers called?

5. What is Grint and Aresko's job?

6. What colour is the Inquisitor's lightsaber?

7. Which is the most powerful ship in the Imperial navy?

8. Who works for the secret police?

9. What is the name of the Inquisitor's spaceship?

10. Which special power can the Inquisitor feel?

Answers on page 45

Glossary

Empire
A group of worlds ruled by an Emperor.

Fleet
A group of spacecraft.

Jedi
Beings who use the Force to help others
in the galaxy.

Lightsaber
Weapon used by Jedi and others who can
feel the Force.

Lures
Tempts a person to do something.

Minerals
Something valuable that is
found in the earth.

Rebellion
A group of people not
following the rules.

Index

Agent Kallus 25, 26–27

Chopper 13

Commandant Aresko 18

Empire 5, 9, 10, 12, 14,
    20–21, 22, 25, 28, 35

Ezra 12, 34–35

Force 20, 32

Hera 12

Imperial Academy 18–19

Inquisitor 4–5, 6–7,
    11, 14, 25, 26, 29,
    32, 36, 38–39, 40–41

Jedi 5, 7, 11, 12–13,
    20, 25, 26–27, 32–33,
    36, 41

Kanan 13, 36

Lightsaber 6–7, 13, 26

Lothal 8–9, 10, 18–19,
    21, 22, 25, 39

Rebel 10–11, 12, 20,
    26, 36, 39, 41

Sabine 13

Star Destroyer 22

Stormtrooper 12,
    14, 16–17, 18, 21,
    34–35, 39

Taskmaster Grint 18

TIE Advanced
    29, 30–31

TIE fighter 12, 28, 31

Utapau 5

Zeb 12

Answers to the quiz on pages 42 and 43:
1. Utapau 2. The Jedi 3. Lothal 4. Stormtroopers
5. Training stormtrooper cadets 6. Red 7. Star Destroyer
8. Agent Kallus 9. TIE Advanced 10. The Force

Guide for Parents

DK Reads is a three-level reading series for children, developing the habit of reading widely for both pleasure and information. These books have exciting running text interspersed with a range of reading genres to suit your child's reading ability, as required by the school curriculum. Each book is designed to develop your child's reading skills, fluency, grammar awareness and comprehension in order to build confidence and engagement when reading.

Ready for a *Beginning to Read* book
YOUR CHILD SHOULD

- be using phonics, including combinations of consonants, such as bl, gl and sm, to read unfamiliar words; and common word endings, such as plurals, ing, ed and ly.

- be using the storyline, illustrations and the grammar of a sentence to check and correct their own reading.

- be pausing briefly at commas, and for longer at full stops; and altering his/her expression to respond to question, exclamation and speech marks.

A Valuable and Shared Reading Experience

For many children, reading requires much effort but adult participation can make this both fun and easier. So here are a few tips on how to use this book with your child.

TIP 1 Check out the contents together before your child begins

- Read the text about the book on the back cover.

- Read through and discuss the contents page together to heighten your child's interest and expectation.

- Briefly discuss any unfamiliar or difficult words on the contents page.

- Chat about the non-fiction reading features used in the book, such as headings, captions, recipes, lists or charts.

This introduction helps to put your child in control and makes the reading challenge less daunting.

TIP 2 Support your child as he/she reads the story pages:

- Give the book to your child to read and turn the pages.

- Where necessary, encourage your child to break a word into syllables, sound out each one and then flow the syllables together. Ask him/her to reread the sentence to check the meaning.

- When there's a question mark or an exclamation mark, encourage your child to vary his/her voice as he/she reads the sentence. Demonstrate how to do this if it is helpful.

TIP 3 Praise, share and chat:

- The factual pages tend to be more difficult than the story pages, and are designed to be shared with your child.

- Ask questions about the text and the meaning of the words used. Ask your child to suggest his/her own quiz questions. These help to develop comprehension skills and awareness of the language used.

A FEW ADDITIONAL TIPS

- Try and read together every day. Little and often is best. After 10 minutes, only keep going if your child wants to read on.

- Always encourage your child to have a go at reading difficult words by themselves. Praise any self-corrections, for example, "I like the way you sounded out that word and then changed the way you said it, to make sense."

- Read other books of different types to your child just for enjoyment and information.

Have you read these other great books from DK?

BEGINNING TO READ

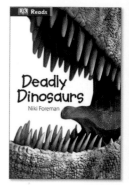

Meet a band of rebels, brave enough to take on the Empire!

Discover the amazing animal tribes living in the land of Chima™.

Roar! Thud! Meet the dinosaurs. Who do you think is the deadliest?

STARTING TO READ ALONE

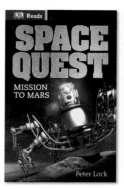

Meet the heroes of Chima™ and help them find the Legend Beasts.

Meet the sharks who live on the reef or come passing through.

Embark on a mission to explore the solar system. First stop – Mars.